Written By

Gary Rap

THE ADVENTURES OF CAPTAIN LANTUS

Created By

Max Rapson

This book is dedicated
to our son Max.

-

When he was only 18 months old
he was diagnosed with type 1 diabetes.
Max was given an insulin pump
to help control his blood sugars
and at the age of just six
he wanted to share an idea
that would inspire children
with Diabetes to feel

like a superhero!

Published in association with Bear With Us Productions

Written By
Gary Rapson

Created By
Max Rapson

Ilustrated By
Eduardo Paj

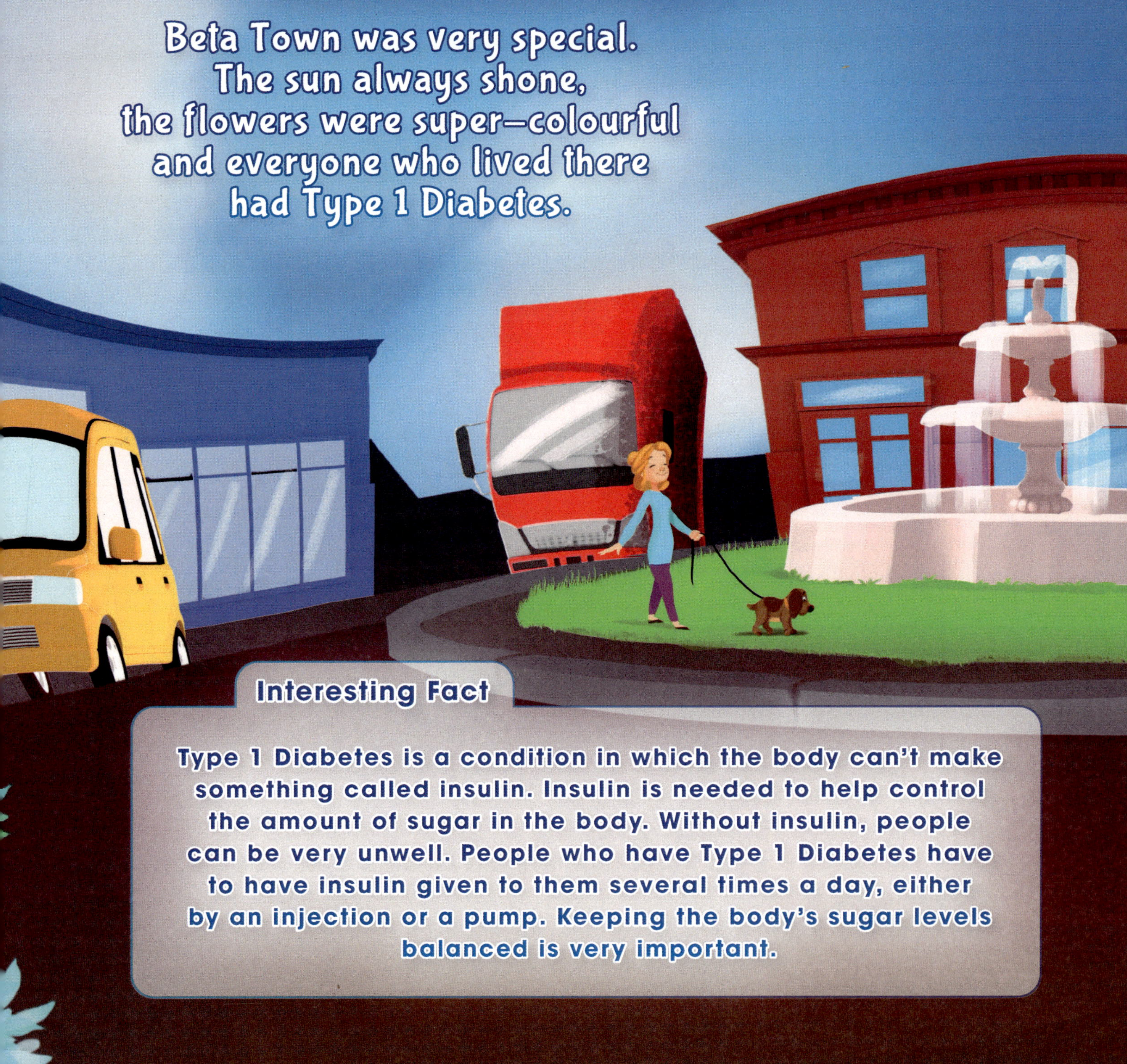

Beta Town was very special. The sun always shone, the flowers were super-colourful and everyone who lived there had Type 1 Diabetes.

Interesting Fact

Type 1 Diabetes is a condition in which the body can't make something called insulin. Insulin is needed to help control the amount of sugar in the body. Without insulin, people can be very unwell. People who have Type 1 Diabetes have to have insulin given to them several times a day, either by an injection or a pump. Keeping the body's sugar levels balanced is very important.

There was something else special about Beta Town.
Right in the centre of town, inside a building,
was a magical cube that had to be guarded day and night.

"What is the cube for?"

a little boy called Max asked his dad one day.

"The Insulin Cube?"

His father looked towards the building where it was kept.

"That cube keeps all of us well. It gives us energy and makes sure our blood sugars stay at the level they are supposed to be. Without it, we would get very sick."

"Wow!"

Max gazed at the building and tried to imagine what the cube looked like. He had heard that it was every colour of the rainbow and it glittered like treasure.

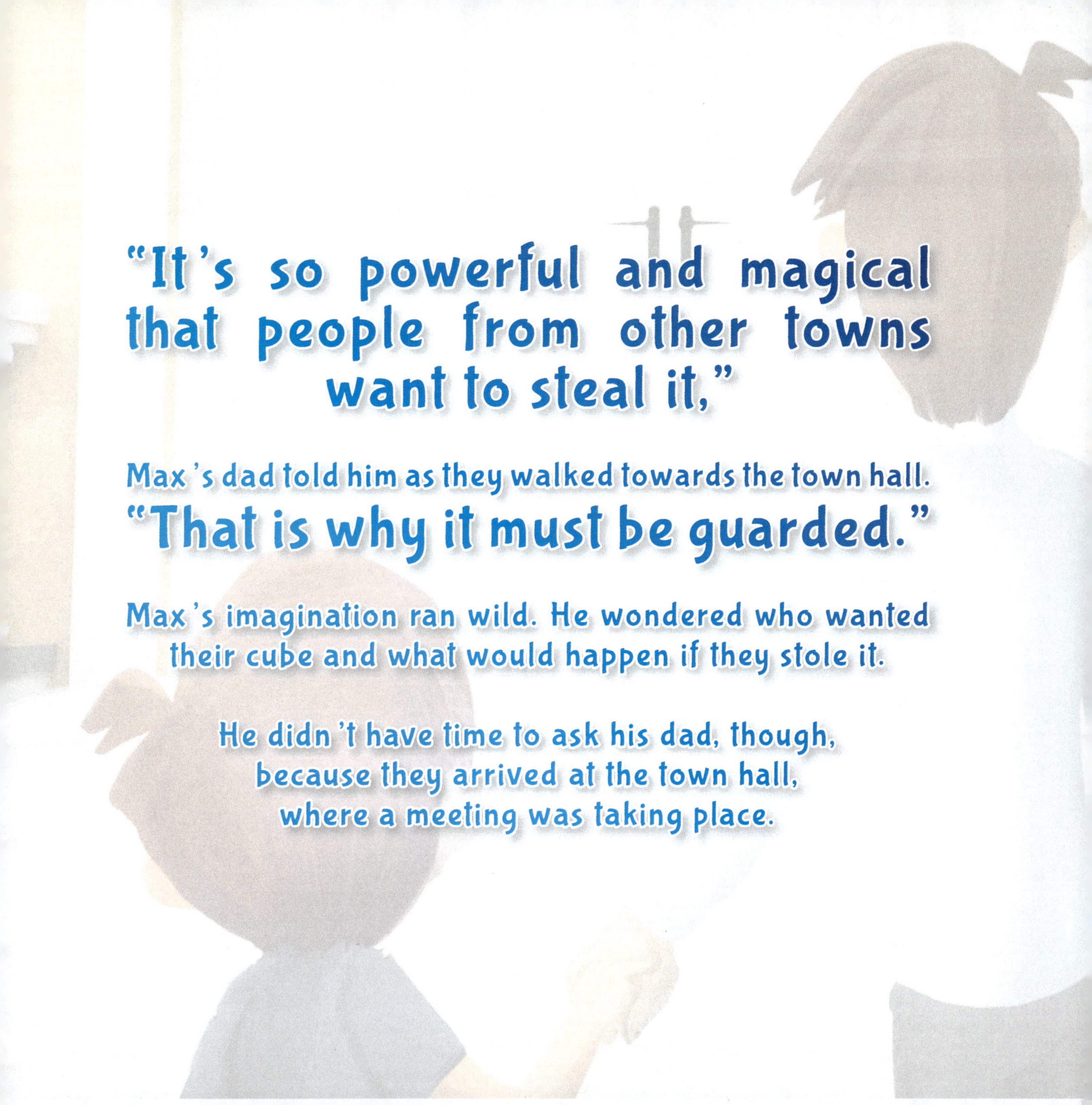

"It's so powerful and magical that people from other towns want to steal it,"

Max's dad told him as they walked towards the town hall.

"That is why it must be guarded."

Max's imagination ran wild. He wondered who wanted their cube and what would happen if they stole it.

He didn't have time to ask his dad, though, because they arrived at the town hall, where a meeting was taking place.

"I have a special announcement!"
Mayor Bolus announced to the gathered crowds.

"Tomorrow, we shall have a food festival! There will be every flavour of ice-cream you can imagine, chocolate fountains and the biggest fruit kebabs in the world! We'll have fairground rides, music and entertainers..."

It sounded amazing. Max grew excited. He was grateful that the cube was there keeping them all safe so they could enjoy the festival without worrying about their insulin or sugar levels.

He couldn't wait to try one of the world's biggest fruit kebabs and maybe dip it into the chocolate fountain.

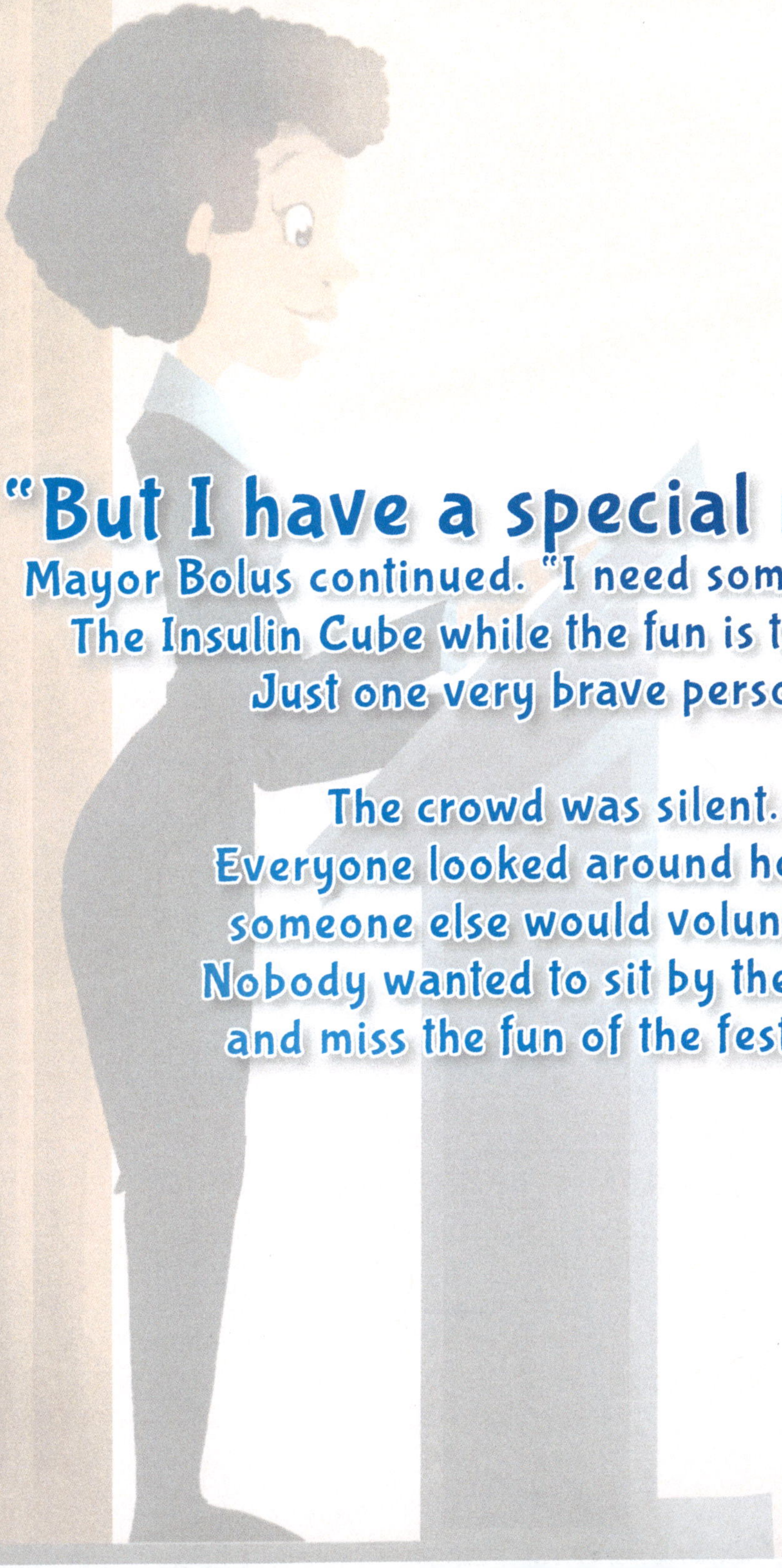

"But I have a special request," Mayor Bolus continued. "I need someone to guard The Insulin Cube while the fun is taking place. Just one very brave person."

The crowd was silent. Everyone looked around hoping someone else would volunteer. Nobody wanted to sit by the cube and miss the fun of the festival.

Max remembered his father telling him about people
from other towns who wanted to steal it.

Someone has to do it. If nobody guards it,
we could all get ill, he thought.

Very bravely, Max raised his hand and said,
"I 'll do it."

Max 's dad smiled at him
and raised him up onto his shoulders proudly.

Everyone cheered and thanked him.

ATTACK
PLAN

"Look at this!"

King Carb, the leader of Town Carb, held up a leaflet.

"Beta Town is having a food festival! This is the perfect chance for us to steal their magical cube!"

King Carb's men, the Carbonites, gathered around him.

"They will be having so much fun they won't notice us sneak in and take the cube! It's worth more than gold! I will be the richest, most powerful person in the world!"

The King laughed wickedly and his men began to plot.

The next morning, Max felt a mixture of excitement and nerves in his tummy.

He was excited to see what the cube looked like at last, but he was also nervous.

What if he didn't guard it well enough?

"You will do a grand job."
His father smiled at him as they walked into town.

Music was already playing, colourful bunting hung from trees and balloons were tied to the park railings.

"You are very brave and very kind to guard the cube rather than have fun at the festival."

"Good morning, Max!"
the mayor greeted him by the building.

Max said goodbye to his dad and stepped into the big, grand building where the cube was kept.

He looked around and was amazed.
The cube sat in the middle of the room,
with bright glittery rays of light shining from it.

"It's even more magical than I had imagined,"
Max said in awe and looked around the room.

"What's in the shiny cupboard?"

Mayor Bolus followed Max's gaze to the golden cupboard at the far end of the room.

She hesitated then whispered,

"Inside is a top-secret new invention.

It's a special pump that can be used instead of the cube. It's not been fully tested yet so nobody knows about it."

"Except for you?"

Max asked.

"And now you,"

Mayor Bolus nodded.

"I'm sure I can trust you not to tell the secret?"

"Of course!" Max insisted.

"I must go now. But remember, all you have to do is sit by the cube and watch the door. If you see the door open, press this emergency button and help will come,"

Mayor Bolus told him and left.

Max sat by the cube and kept his eyes on the door. As the morning went by, the room was filled with the sound of laughter and cheers from outside.

"Everyone is having such a great time,"

Max smiled.

"All thanks to the cube keeping them well and me guarding it."

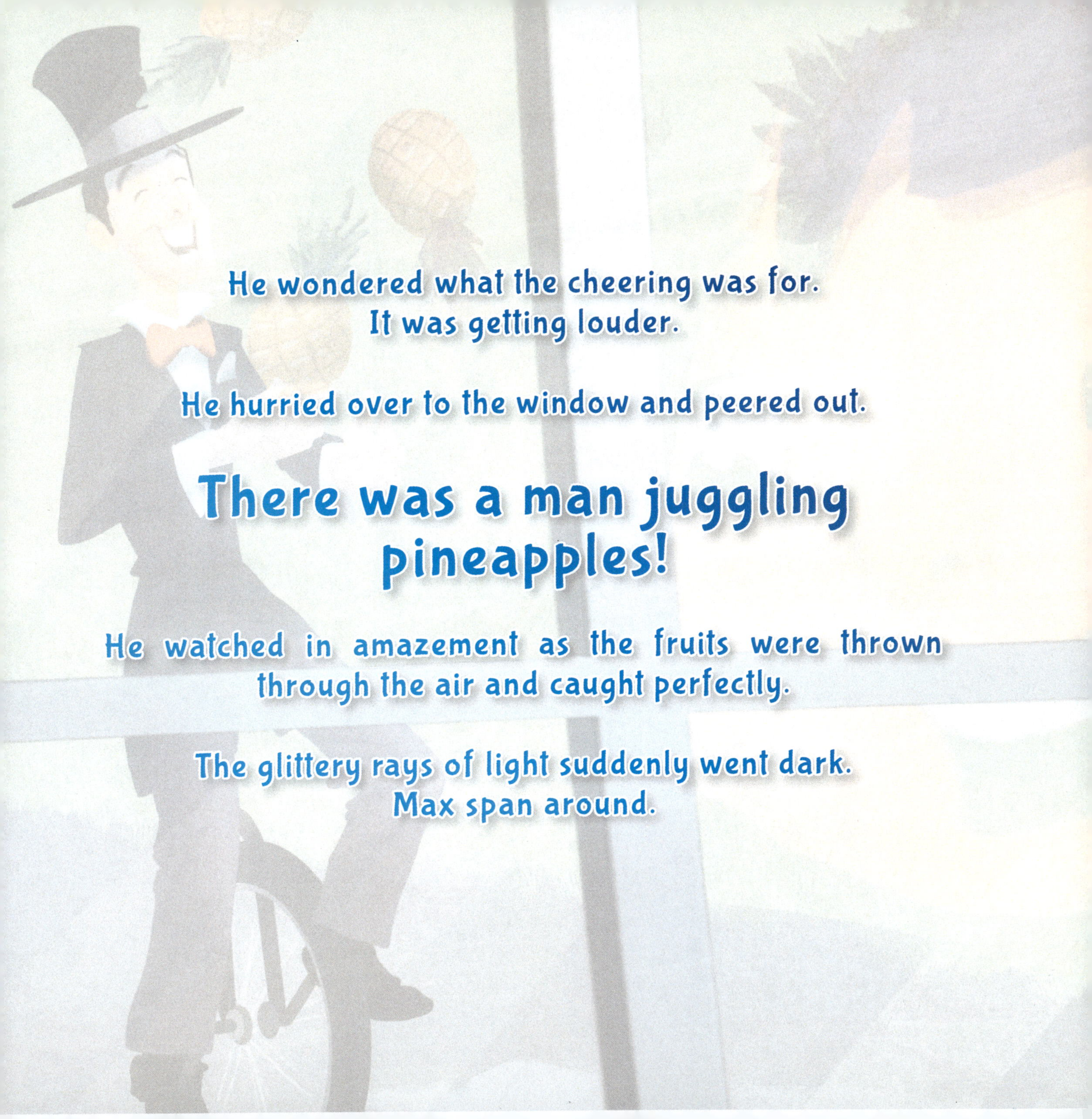

He wondered what the cheering was for.
It was getting louder.

He hurried over to the window and peered out.

There was a man juggling pineapples!

He watched in amazement as the fruits were thrown through the air and caught perfectly.

The glittery rays of light suddenly went dark.
Max span around.

"Oh no! The cube!"
he shouted as he saw the Carbonites snatching it
and hurrying towards the door.
"Stop!"

"It is King Carb 's now!"
the Carbonites shouted.

Max tried to grab the cube back,
but the Carbonites were too strong for him.

They flung him to the floor and fled.
Max lay where the cube had been
and felt his energy draining from him.
Hours passed and the sounds from outside were changing.

"Everyone is ill and it's all my fault,"

Max cried. He had to find a way to help.

Then he remembered the golden cupboard and the top-secret pump.

He struggled to his feet and stumbled over to the cupboard.

With nerves jangling all through his body, he opened the door.

Max grabbed the pump from inside and quickly attached it to his stomach. He waited... and waited some more... and then...

"Wow!"

Max felt his body changing
as energy filled him up.

He started spinning round
and round until a cloak flew out
behind him. His body began to
glow and, looking down,

he saw he was wearing
the most incredible outfit.

Captain Lantus,
a new superhero,
was born!

Max didn't stop to admire his transformation.
Instead, he lifted his arms high,

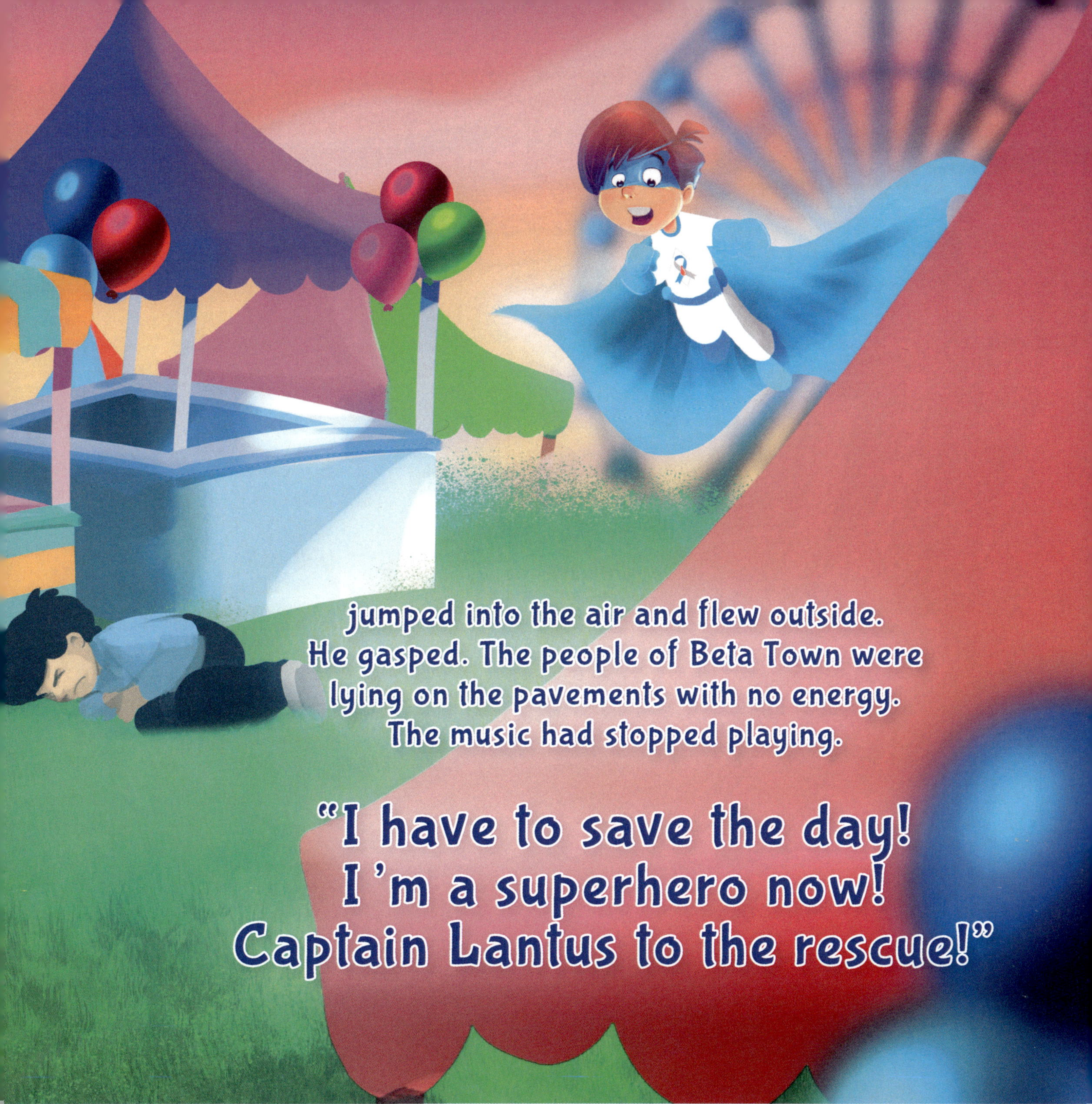

jumped into the air and flew outside. He gasped. The people of Beta Town were lying on the pavements with no energy. The music had stopped playing.

"I have to save the day! I'm a superhero now! Captain Lantus to the rescue!"

He flew as fast as he could towards Carb Town, catching up with the Carbonites on top of a hill.

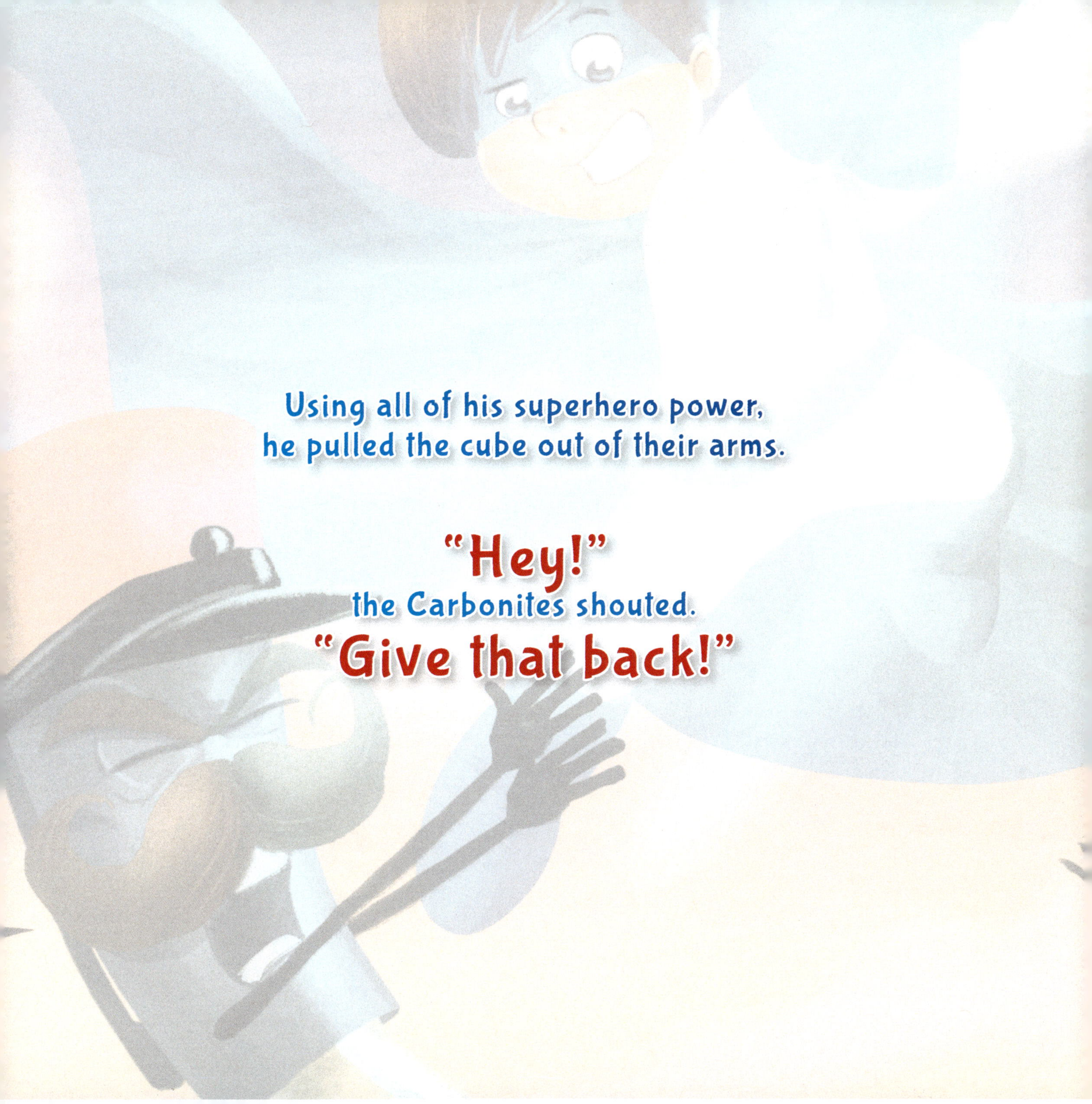

Using all of his superhero power,
he pulled the cube out of their arms.

"Hey!"
the Carbonites shouted.
"Give that back!"

But Captain Lantus was more powerful than all the Carbonites put together.

He flew back to the cube room, faster than a shooting star, and placed the cube back where it belonged.

Captain Lantus watched as the brightly coloured rays began to shine from the cube again.

He peered out of the window and saw people standing up, stretching and smiling.

They were better!

Captain Lantus spun round and round and round until...

he was a Seven-year-old boy again.

People rushed into the cube room to join him.

"What happened?
We all felt ill..."
His father was by his side.

"We thought something had happened to the cube,"
the mayor explained.

"I saw the face of a superhero
in the window!"
another person cried.

"Nope, no superhero here,
just me."
Max smiled.

"I think it's time you enjoyed the festival now," Mayor Bolus said, winking at Max.

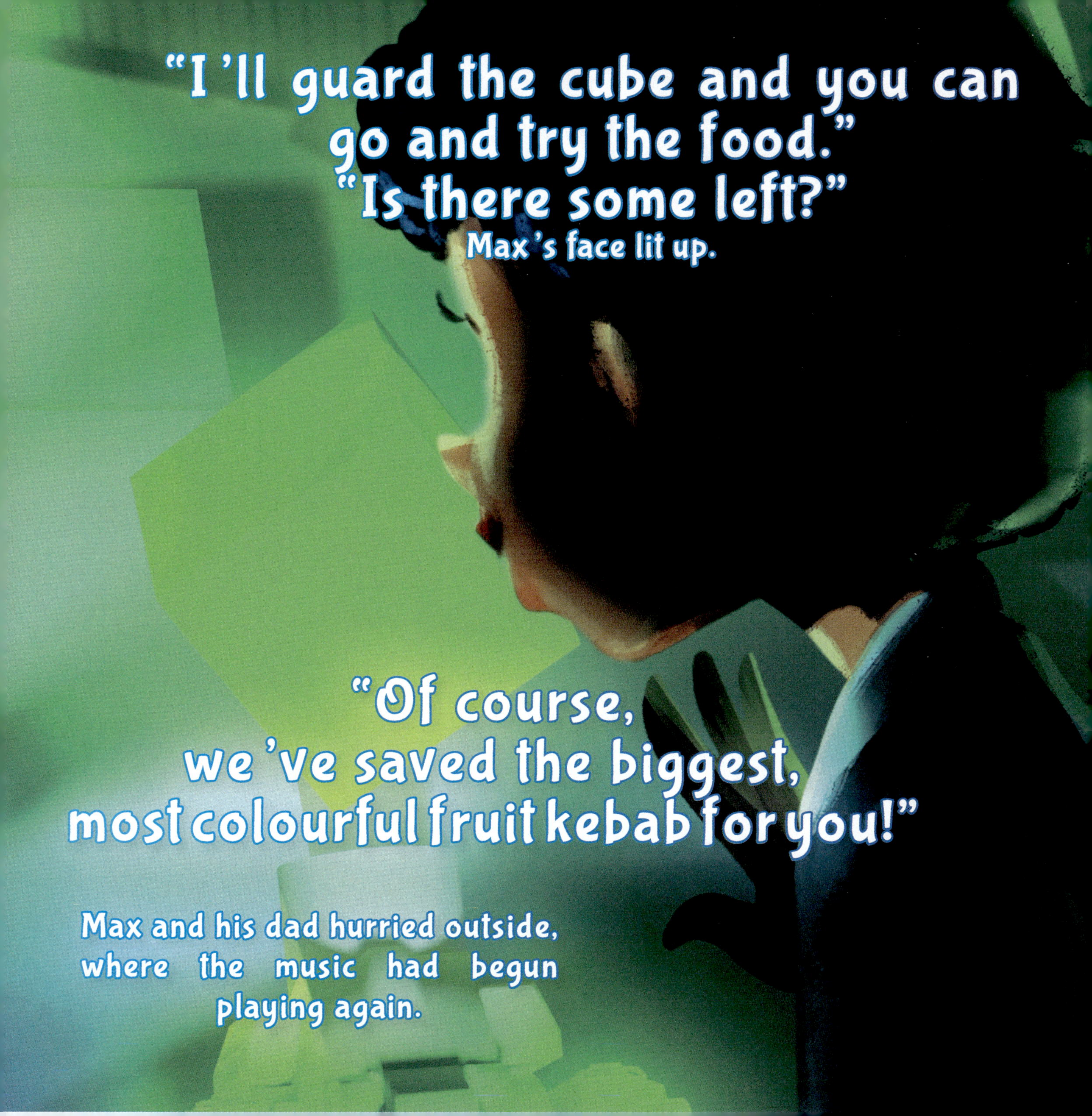

"I'll guard the cube and you can go and try the food."

"Is there some left?"

Max's face lit up.

"Of course, we've saved the biggest, most colourful fruit kebab for you!"

Max and his dad hurried outside, where the music had begun playing again.

"Did you see a superhero in there?"
his father asked, handing him the most amazing fruit kebab Max had ever seen.

"Nope."
Max dipped the kebab into the chocolate fountain. He felt the pump still attached to his tummy and smiled.

Captain Lantus would remain his secret.

WILL RETURN!

Made in the USA
Las Vegas, NV
20 November 2020